DEATH'S PROMISE

STARK LOVE · BOOK 1

To order additional copies of this book, contact:
Xlibris
844-714-8691
www.Xlibris.com
Orders@Xlibris.com

ISBN: Softcover 979-8-3694-1942-7
Hardcover 979-8-3694-1939-7
EBook 979-8-3694-1940-3

Library of Congress Control Number: 2024907073

Print information available on the last page

Rev. date: 04/10/2024

WHAT FUELS FRIVOLITY IS

1

CLAWING OUT WITH NO CLAUSE

*

The earth has become a quantum nightmare in the wake of the nuclear war that decimated most of its lifeforms. A phenomenon known as the "scatter," caused by omnipresent radiation, destroys identification when observed; fingerprints, blood types, and DNA codes shift and rearrange.

*

THE DARKNESS IT UNDERMINES

Exiting her apartment onto the battered street, a twenty-seven-year-old girl named 9 walks with her eyes down. This part of New York City is populated mostly by robots and is notorious for abundant drug trading. Before her, not unusual, an unconscious figure is slumped against a pile of trash bags. But another dark figure is there as well. Curled up around him is a vampire whose fangs are embedded deep into his neck. At the sound of approaching footsteps, the vampire withdraws into darkness.

The vampire, Molly, feels like she's dreaming. That girl who had just passed by had an energy aura that was fresh and sweet; different from humans here on earth. Curiosity overtakes her. She begins following 9, silent. When 9 reaches her convertible car and perches up on the back of it, debating what to do with her evening, the vampire approaches. Aside from her long fangs and black eyes, Molly looks like a human. She appears to be around 9's age. Though a vampire's fangs are retractable Molly can't contain her excitement, and so with fangs exposed Molly speaks, "Hi."

No response comes, though, for 9 is deaf. After a vacant stare down and awkward pause, Molly takes 9's hand and greets her psychically. 9 is surprised to hear the vampire's voice in her head—she had only ever been able to have this kind of communication with animals. Molly invites 9 to a discotheque, and 9 happily agrees. She hops into 9's convertible and they make their way there.

In the club's parking garage, Molly hands 9 a small candy and says psychically, "*This is spiderplant sap.*" The candy melts like crystalized maple syrup in 9's mouth. Almost immediately, shimmering rainbows begin to decorate the already highly graffitied walls.

They enter the club through a back door into a private tearoom on the second floor. The walls are glowing. Palm trees slathered in coconut oil begin to erupt up through the floor tiles and rip through couches in sprays of neon dirt. The club is morphing into a form not possible within earth's dimensionality.

In an adjacent room, a pig-headed man stuck in a drug trance has been leaning against the wall. As the walls start to glow they become extremely hot. He awakens in a panic squealing, face scalded and chest burnt open. High on the second story balcony, muddled with confusion, he blindly runs out of his room and flips up over the guardrail. Melting entrails go flying as his body plummets into the crowd.

Molly and 9 hear the pig-man's squeal and leave their tearoom to investigate. While they peer over the balcony to see the wreckage, another pig-man in a different room has also suddenly snapped out of his drug-induced trance. Spurred on by violent excitement, he bursts out of his room. Upon seeing the bums of two pretty girls, he shrieks and grasps wildly for them. But the momentum of his body's weight as he runs forward overcomes him, and he ends up shoving 9 over the balcony guardrail like how the first pig fell.
twitch
But 9's fate was not to be the same. As she goes careening over she flips like a cat. Claws hidden beneath her skin slice slits between her shoulders, rapidly releasing folded wings that snap open to catch her.

9 lands a tad ungracefully on the floor. Furthering the night's confusion, surrounding her are animal-humanoid ravers. Though on earth some people have animal ears and tails, she had never seen anything like this. Molly comes down the stairs quickly after 9. When the vampire reaches her, Molly has goat horns protruding from her head. She is glad 9 is unhurt. And as for those horns, 9 doesn't question anything; they just dance.

Meanwhile the fallen pig-man has disintegrated into a slimy puddle of purple jelly. Something glints on the surface of the puddle, catching 9's eye. The slime reaches up like a blooming flower as 9 leans in for a closer look. It then presents her with a halo, which she gently takes.

But then, a magnetic force drags the halo from 9's hand up toward the ceiling. A three-tailed black jackal bursts out. As it flies through the air, the halo implodes behind it and a wormhole opens in front of it. The jackal disappears into the wormhole, leaving 9 and Molly standing there in confusion.

The night gets stranger. Nearby, a chubby wolf-headed man pulls out an impossibly huge sandwich from his comparatively small waist pack. Watching with jealous eyes, his wolf-headed friend suddenly lunges for it! But as the sandwich wolf is punched off his feet, he spitefully throws the sandwich into the air, further enraging the other. From the sandwich emerges a salmon of sorrow, spewing a froth that rains down on them both.

The salmon's froth melts away their wolf-head flesh like acid, revealing their true forms—pigs! ‌bashed by his appearance, the larger of the two boars uses a malware program installed in his brain ɔ whip up a spell, and suddenly his fat belly shrinks to look chiseled and fit. But by using the malware najik inside the club, the pigs' presence has been detected by universal authority. Police alarms blare inside their brains. As fugitives wanted for illegal intergalactic activities, the pigs have to leave fast! ‌arty over! Ditching his friends, Boorish the boar leaps into his full animal form. Utilizing his malware by spouting some strange spoken symbols, he melts a hole into the floor, and jumps in.

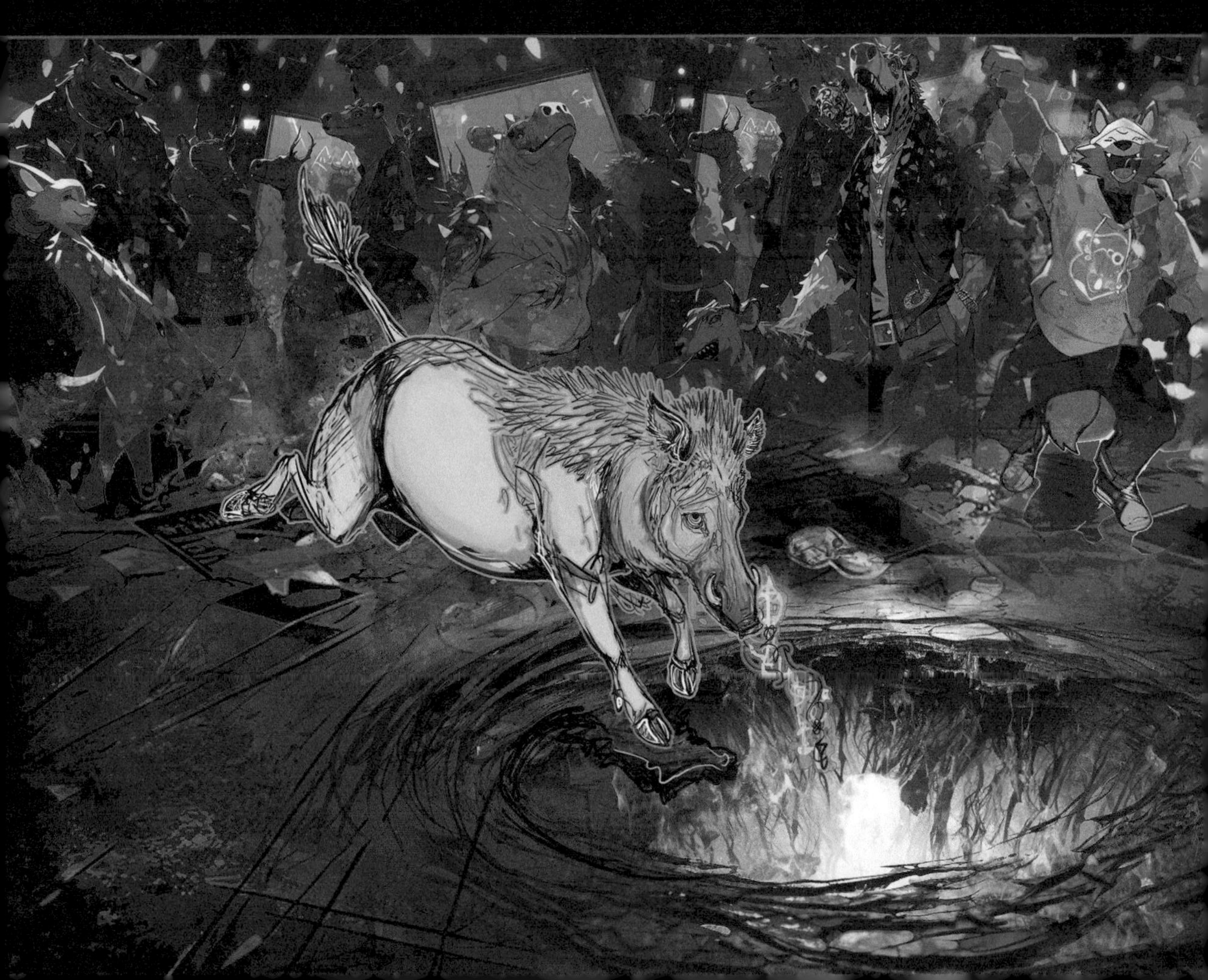

Behind 9 comes a loud buzzing—the reason why Boorish and his buddies were here tonight. The huge beetle they had planted in the club has a herculean horn with a swan head on the end. It descends from the ceiling, making a beeline to 9. Although 9 puts up her wings like a shield, the bug is freaky fast. As it whips around 9, its swan-head-horn knocks Molly to the ground. The bug's pincers bite into 9's spine at the base of her neck. A piercing ring splinters out from the bite, escalating into a tone that sends shockwaves of energy through the club.

A burning bright light emanates out of 9 as she collapses onto the beetle, snapping its horn in half. 9's energy aura has shattered. Molly gasps as a smoke-like material rises up out of 9; she grabs hold of it. Had 9 not been here at the club, this wouldn't have—shouldn't have—happened. In the same instant, a four-eared rabbit springs out of the cracked-open beetle horn. Molly is shocked to see it here but hasn't the time to think. She squeezes her eyes shut. With one arm she throws the liquid-smoke like a rope lasso to catch the rabbit's foot, and with the other she takes 9's hand. The rabbit goes right through the ceiling as the venue is overtaken by the explosion of 9's light energy.

When Molly opens her eyes she is somewhat confused. The rabbit is gone. She and 9 are sitting at a picnic table on the Coney Island boardwalk, a few miles from the Brooklyn club. 9 is dead. Though rather than departing for the Afterlife, she's here in limbo; stuck inside her dead body and only partially conscious. For better or worse, something inside Molly had told her to hold on to 9's spirit-soul (taiji) in 9's moment of death.

In the Afterlife, it is illegal for a dead being to interfere with or alter the course of a mortal's life.

Dragging 9’s taiji behind her, Molly leads 9 into the ocean. They go for so long that 9 feels herself beginning to drown. Despite her pleading for some kind of explanation, Molly keeps going without saying a word. The water gets rougher and rougher. Finally, 9 loses all her strength and falls limp.

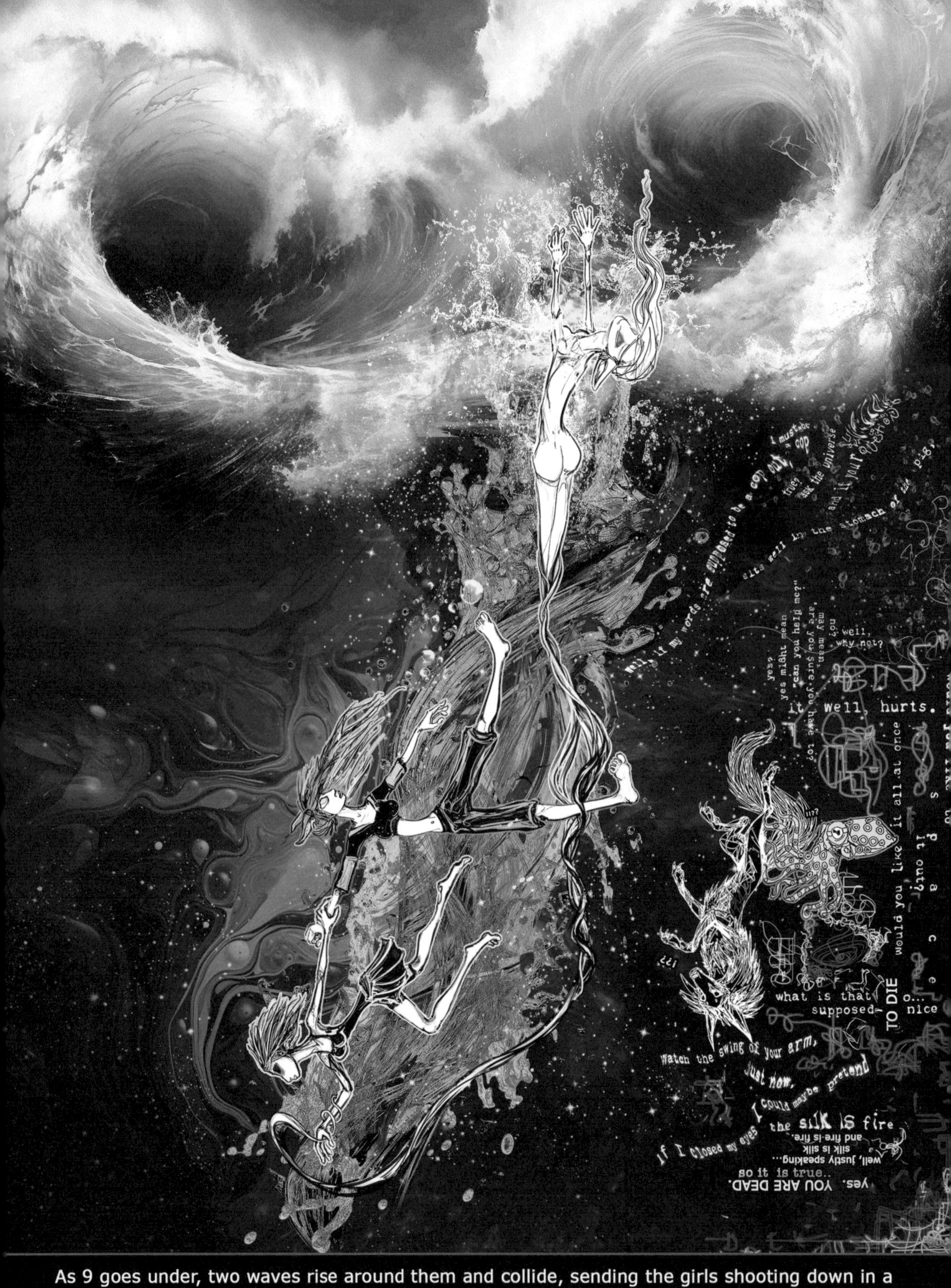

As 9 goes under, two waves rise around them and collide, sending the girls shooting down in a jet-stream. Molly had drowned 9's semi-conscious body intentionally. Only at 9's drowning point

The vortex brings the girls straight into the lair of a dolphin. He's surprised to see them, knowing the conditions it takes to find him. Speaking to their minds, he inquires, *"Back again I see Molly... and now who might this be?"* Molly, uncertainly, *"The angel."* Like when taking a sip of your coffee while hearing something that makes you spit it back out in surprise, a big bubble comes out of the dolphin, Yayo's, blow hole. Yayo: *"Oh my! Let's go, no Time to waste..."* He had quickly ascertained the situation, seeing 9's taiji. And he knew what to do.

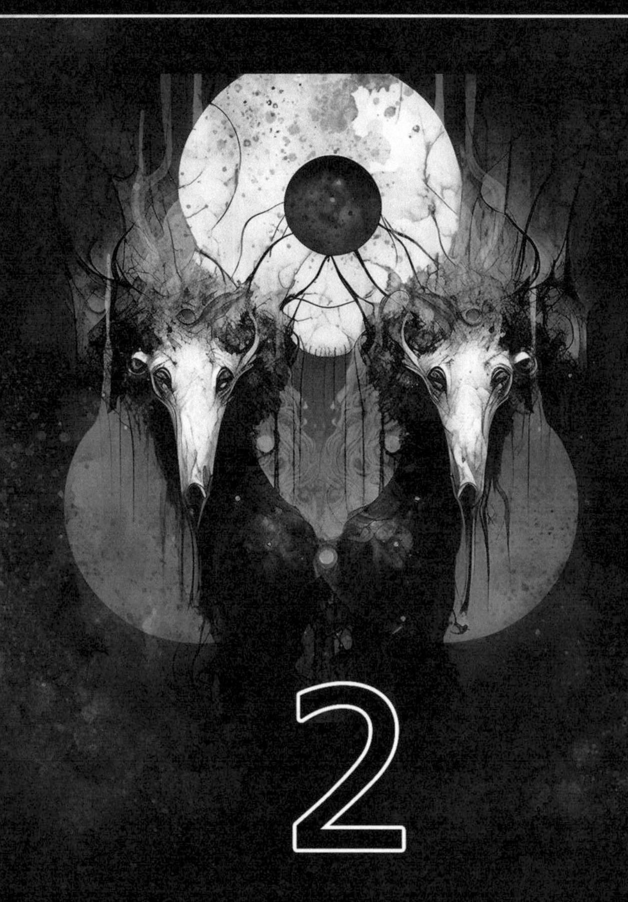

2

ANOTHER SUN

*

In this universe there are three levels

1. THE PHYSICAL UNIVERSE

2. THE DREAM WORLD

3. THE AFTERLIFE

*

After dying, all beings go to the Afterlife. Dying doesn't change who you are inside. But upon entering the Afterlife, a being's soul and spirit reboot a new vessel (body). Since there is no aging past a body's prime in the Afterlife, if you die as a kid, you will wake up as a dead kid and grow to be a dead adult. If you die old, you wake up dead old and your age reverses until your body is again in its prime. Here in the Afterlife, there are infinitely spectacular landscapes, both wild and civilized. But it is not a heaven in any traditional sense; there is as much darkness here as there is eternal bliss.

The dead can harness a mysterious force known as majik. Every complete being—one with a body, soul, and spirit—has a universal ranking order (URO) number, which has either a positive (+) charge or a negative (-). The power of your majik is determined by the absolute value of your URO number; the closer to zero it is, the more powerful you are. The most powerful being in the universe is URO number one: the blue-ringed octopus Dr.8.

"Time" is different in the Afterlife. Time is a physical material—a black, reddish liquid. Time can be used to do things with, like as a fuel or tool. Because of this, Time is also the Afterlife's currency (money). Surrounding the River of Time, the source of all Time in the Afterlife, is ScarCity. ScarCity is dense and crowded. It is the biggest city in the Afterlife, and grows constantly, just as the River of Time does.

Terribly hot fire burns inside of a black dragon resting in a water forest. The forest sits between the ocean surrounding ScarCity's island and the desert that flanks the city. A red dragon has followed him here, desperately trying to win his affections. Dragons are mostly solitary creatures; they come in all shapes and sizes and have all sorts of unique abilities. What defines a dragon is its special organ sack, which creates the powerful force called dragonflame. But the black dragon has a vulnerability—he cannot use his dragonflame. His sack is sealed shut. So instead his fire festers and rots his insides.

The red dragon follows the other dragon across the desert. Today there is to be a great carnival in ScarCity, held every three hundred and twenty-four suns. It had been a very long wait this go-around, as, the length of a sun (day) is not a set number of hours. When the ancient cosmic tigers Tru of light and Vauxen of darkness throw the eternally glowing ball of light around the spherical circumference of the Afterlife, the speed and angle of the pass often varies.

When the two dragons arrive at the carnival grounds there is no music playing, no bright lights, and save for some vultures, no beings. It is painfully obvious that the joyful festivity had gone awry. Among mangled pieces of carnival rides, remnants of bodies litter the ground. The black dragon's frothy dragonflame bubbles up from his nostrils, eliciting a flinching head shake. Despondent, he lies down in the midst of the chaos and closes his eyes. The red dragon looms over him, still, paying no mind to the disaster around them.

Sometime later, the rustling of brooms and bins awakens the black dragon, who had unwittingly fallen asleep in the wake of being tirelessly pursued by the red dragon. As the walrus janitors go about cleaning up the big mess, the black dragon stretches and yawns. His curled-up tongue unfurls, and streams of gold scarab beetles scramble out from underneath, burrowing into the ground.

The other dragon had slept very little. With a tail flick she implores, "Don't you want me?"

But the black dragon snorts, "I do not seek that." As an afterthought, he chortles, "Anyway, I seek only what is true, and that is not you."

Taken aback, the red dragon momentarily stole away from his biting opprobrium and back into her world of anxiety. When she comes to, she hops down off the tossed carousel horse she had perched up on. Without making eye contact, the red dragon sidles up against the black dragon's body. But he does not respond; he simply begins to walk away.

A furious rage seethes within the red dragon as she is left behind. She begins to conjure a curse, stalking the black dragon as he crosses the desert and passes through the water forest. When her curse is ready, she rises onto her hind legs with an arched neck, surging with power. Her evil majik snakes across the ground like lightning, striking the unsuspecting black dragon hard.

The black dragon has no desire to fight back; instead, he runs. But his legs are going numb, his wings won't open, and his bounding strides stiffen. By the time he reaches the ocean shore, his body has hardened so much he's locked in like a statue. When the red dragon finally catches up, only one thing remains moving. Something on his withers is wriggling, emitting a glowing pulse. The red dragon scuttles up his back for a better look. Hiding between locks of his mane is a gemstone scarab beetle.

Immediately, the red dragon grabs the scarab. But the gemstone is attached to the black dragon's spine. Her long clumsy claws skid all over the surface of the stone, ruining its delicate details. When it finally snaps off, the scarab is but an un-molded lump. Smugly clutching her prize, the red dragon puts her nose to her belly and breathes in hard. Her entire body is slurped up in through her nostrils; she vanishes.

A ceaseless flow of liquified sapphire begins dripping out of the black dragon's eyes. As day becomes night, a whole puddle has formed around his feet. The sound of the gentle waves pushing ashore under the stars that peek through from the physical realm is his only comfort. His body aches, and he drifts in and out of consciousness. When he is fully lost in an abyss similar to a coma, bubbles appear on the surface of the liquified sapphire. Flailing and splashing erratically, a jackal emerges. She staggers to her feet in a trance, trembling uncontrollably.

WHAT FUELS FRIVOLITY IS

3

BARATHRUM

*

DARKNESS HAS TWO FORMS

1. DARK ENERGY

2. DARK MATTER

*

THE DARKNESS IT UNDERMINES

The red dragon, Poqi, retreats with the ruby in her claws to a shabby house sitting on stilts over a swamp of acid. This is the secret base of the ruthless gang of ruffians she leads. The 'Roughnecks,' as they're called, run a mafia so tight that their front has even the highest powers in the Afterlife duped. It goes without saying that all Roughnecks have negative URO numbers.

The only way to enter and exit the premises is through a wormhole portal on a boulder attached to a rope bridge connecting to the front porch. The Farmhaus appears on the outside to have only two floors, but this is an illusion. A majik staircase leads to a limitless number of floors; at present there are about three hundred and eight or so—*however old Molly is…*

Poqi stomps inside and startles awake a war-thog named Feenickz. She callously zaps a majik spell at his forehead, knocking him off his hooves. Poqi: "You and Slothy will go to the Royal Animal Guild castle with this."

As he crumples into a heap, Feenickz the thog croaks, "But Poqi, we are not allowed in there." It is well known that those with negative URO numbers cannot enter that place. Poqi just rolls her eyes and drops the black dragon's ruby onto his back. She then knocks a sloth, Slothy, off a hanging rope with another spell, and wraps an amulet around his wrist.

Because only positive URO number holders can create and store internal majik, negative URO number holders carry with them a (usually cloaked unless depleted) vial containing Time. Using the Time as fuel, they can create majik. But Time is not easy to come by, like any money. The strength of the Roughneck gang comes from their creation of a formula called dirty-Time. Their reserve of Time is fused with corpses they smuggle in from the physical realm to stretch the amount (watering it down, in essence). They produce mass quantities. But dirty-Time is unwieldy and yields strange results when used for majik.

The sloth and thog set out, taking a wormhole trip halfway to their destination. Feenickz levitates the sloth the rest of the way because wormholes are bright and noisy; they would be spotted immediately. Upon arrival, Feenickz deposits Slothy in the brush and wades into the dark liquid Time that surrounds the RAG castle. Slothy, poised and ready, begins chanting a spell. Faster and faster the spell crescendos, coming out of his mouth quicker than he can move it and causing him to slur his words into a madman's jargon.

As the Roughneck sloth swings the amulet rhythmically, the spell takes hold of the castle; a sonic boom blasts through the castle walls. Asleep inside, Gravity the ancient wolf jumps to his paws with a howl.

Gravity turns at the sound of Ipijo the bighorn ram toppling to the ground like a log. Vurrent the ocelot's half-eaten treat drops from her paw. Their bodies have been flash frozen! In the adjacent room, billowing herbal smoke cloaks a group of usually rowdy royals now cast silent and motionless. Seeking an explanation, the wolf makes for the stairwell; the RAG castle's control rooms are all on the ground floor.

Meanwhile, just outside, war-thog Feenickz brazenly pushes the stolen ruby hard against a sapphire scarab beetle lock that seals shut the castle's front door. Writhing beneath the pressure, the befuddled insect's wings release, yielding to the negative URO number holder.

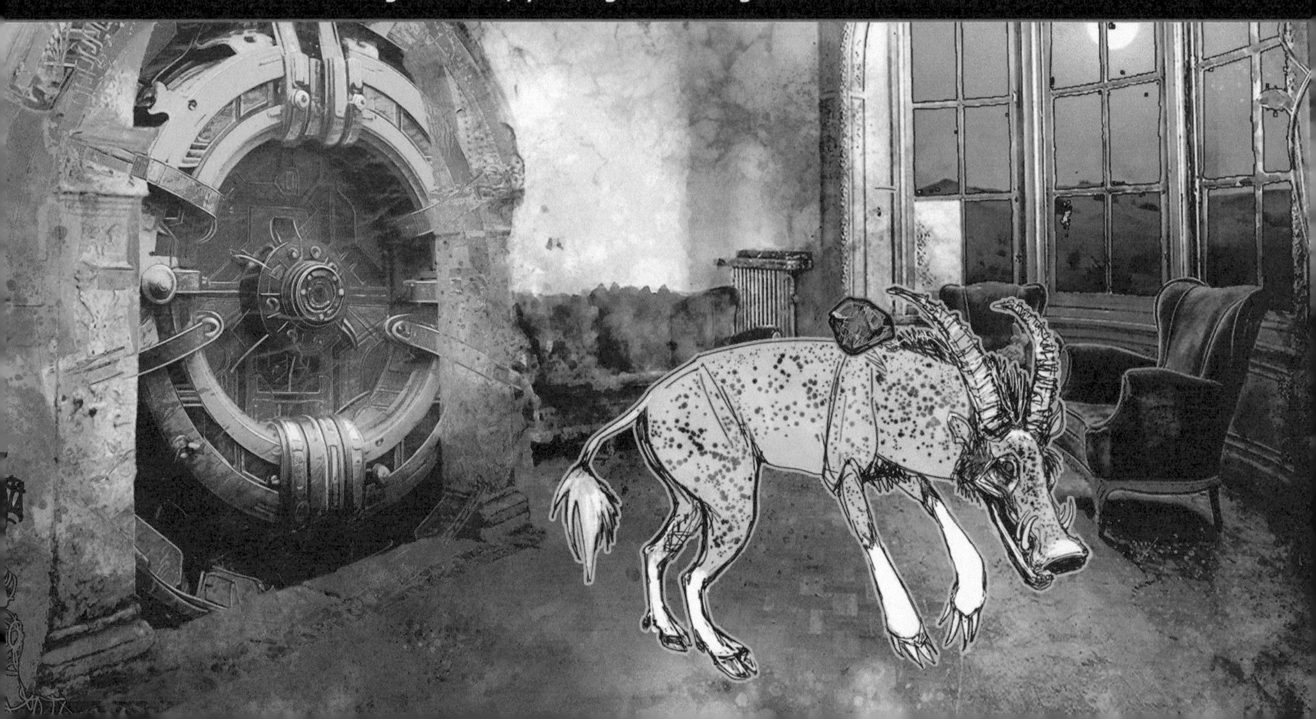

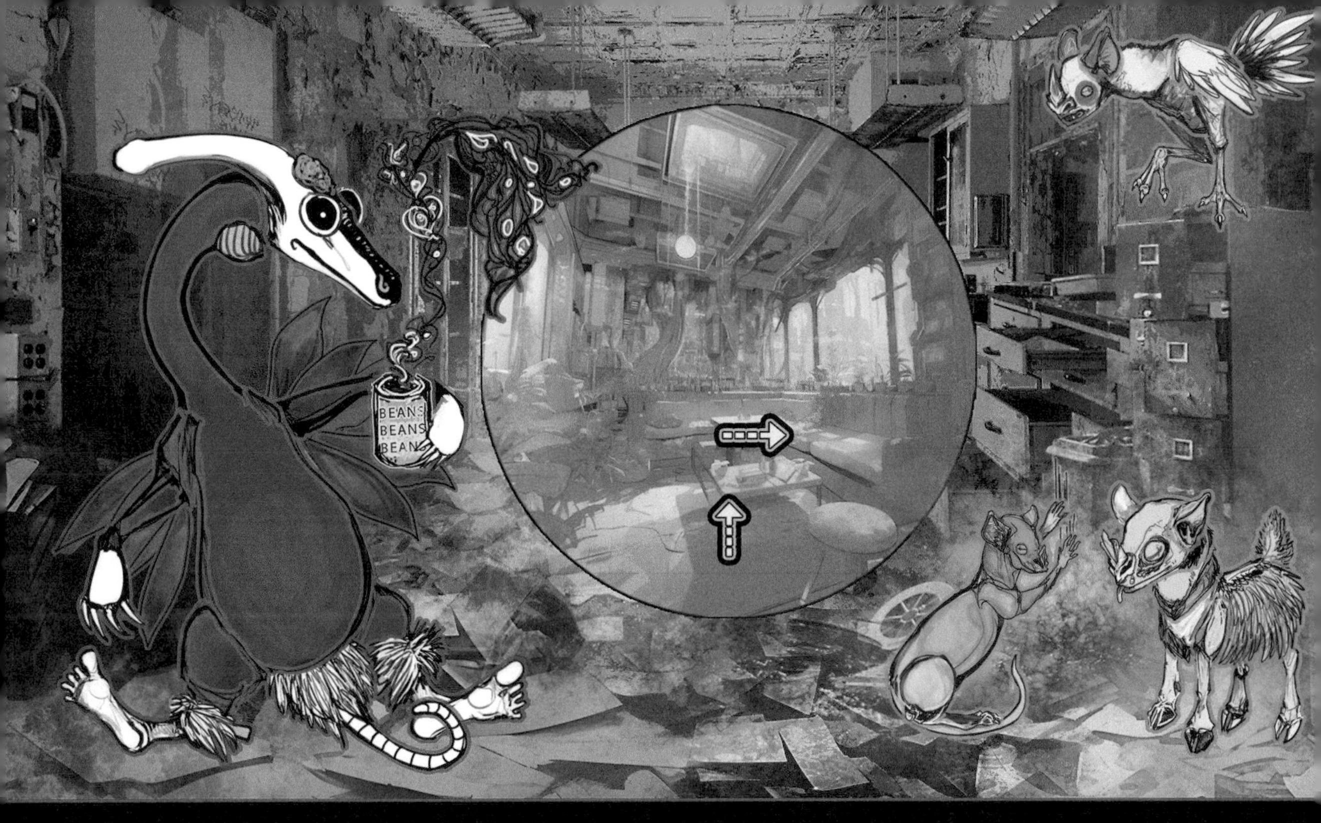

At the Farmhaus, Poqi and a few Roughnecks watch Feenickz from an orb set up to see through his eyes. As Feenickz searches, he bristles against an unexpected warmth. It isn't just warm, actually. This heat is torrid–scathing! The war-thog's negative URO number is causing the immense powers pulsing inside here to smoke and sizzle his skin. They knew they weren't allowed in the RAG castle by formality, but they weren't aware the presiding majik would burn him like a basic (weak) vampire in sunlight.

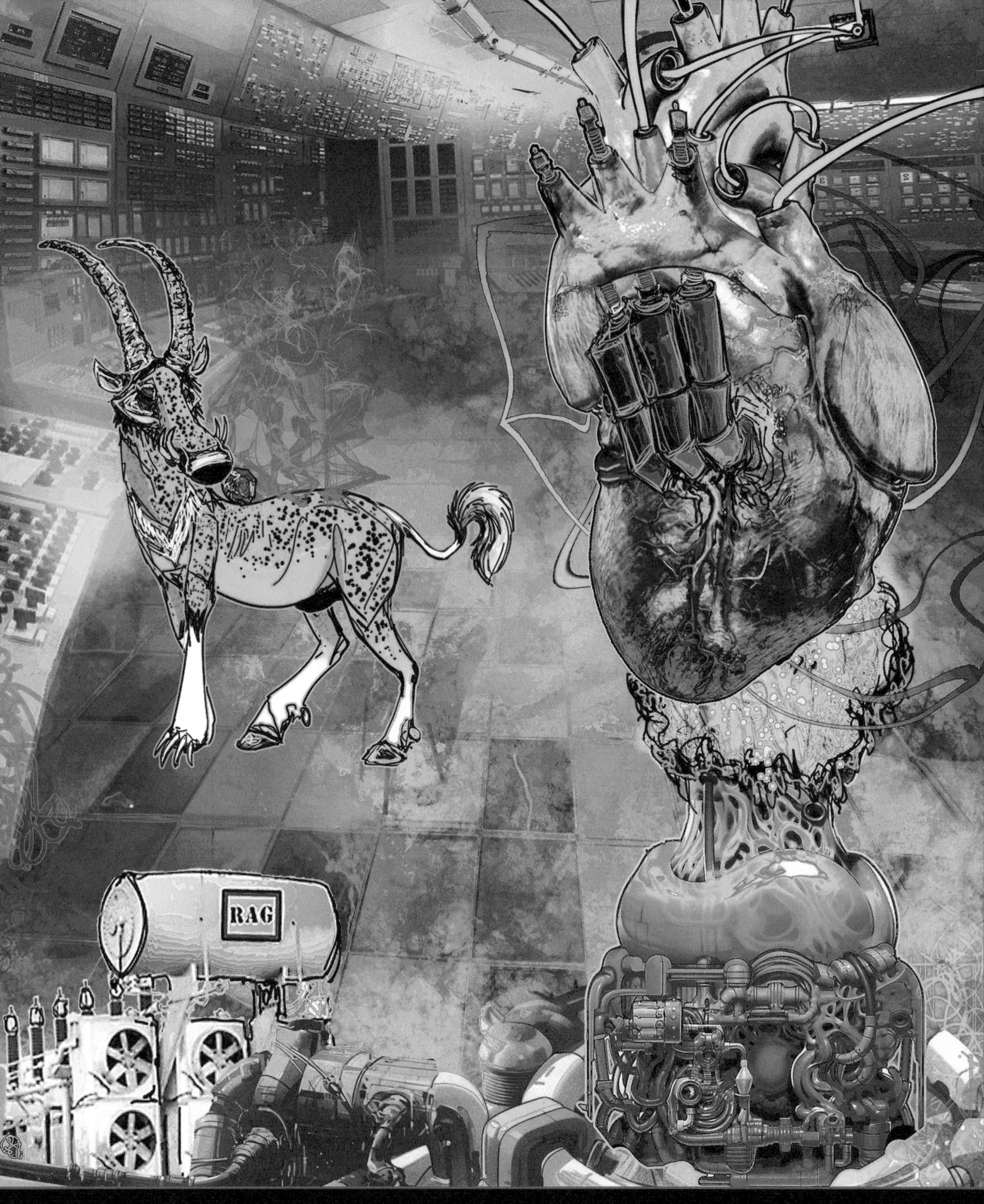

Despite the pain, Feenickz presses on. He comes upon a small room exuding waves of heat. Control panels adorn the room from floor to ceiling, and in the center is a giant heart hooked up to wires and converters. Poqi and the others look at the beating heart with their mouths agape.

Poqi: "This is it—it must be! The RAG heart!" The heart's existence was only a rumor to anyone outside of the Royal Animal Guild. The enigmatic object converts dark energy into dark matter; an unfathomably powerful material that the framework of the entire Dream World is built with. Poqi's eyes gleam with malevolence.

Feenickz approaches the heart. The thog boosts himself up onto a wobbly little cloud made with some dirty-Time majik, and with a claw makes a cut into the flesh. Unapologetically, he shoves the ruby into the slot. The heart shudders. He licks up a rancid purple sludge that oozes out of the gash and then fires up a laser beam from his eye to weld the gap shut. There is no scar.

The smell of cooking bacon wafts into Gravity's nose, growing stronger as the wolf heads down the castle's nine flights of stairs. It's coming from the room of the RAG heart.

A snarling growl from behind sends a shiver down Feenickz's spine. Gravity nearly eats him, but Feenickz hastily activates a pop-up screen on his wrist, stopping Gravity in his tracks. On the screen is the four-eared rabbit crying bubbles for tears. When it was leaping out of the discotheque with Molly and 9, the rabbit was intercepted by Roughnecks. They then rendered the girls unconscious with dirty-Time majik and captured it, dumping Molly and 9 out onto the boardwalk. Affixed to the rabbit's face is a mask that is sucking out its potent majik into a canister.

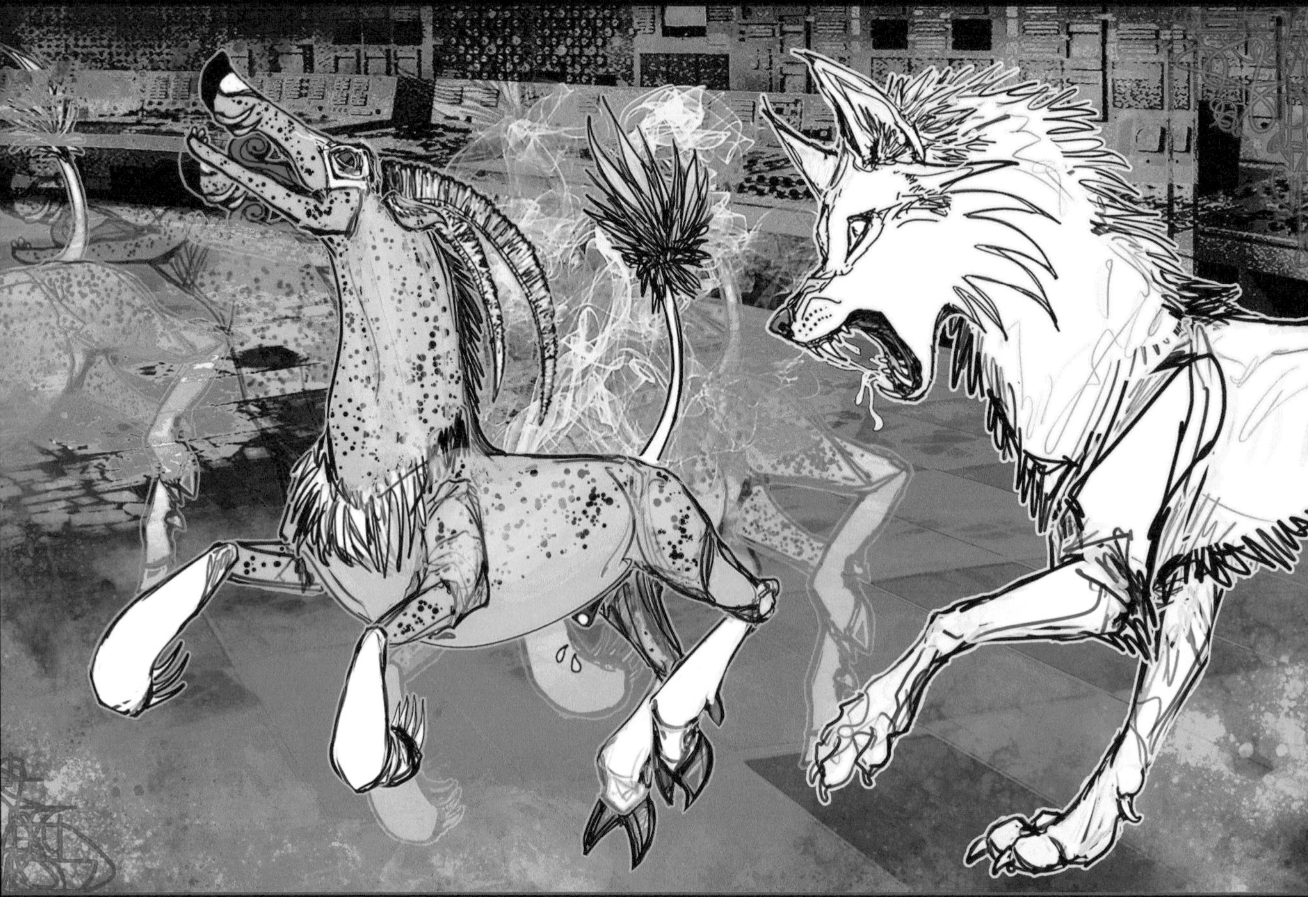

Since the rabbit is being held hostage in an unknown location, the wolf is in a precarious position. Pulses of Gravity's rage shake the castle. The rabbit is his dear Molly's majik pet. LoxRion 28, the high ranking Roughneck in charge of bottling the rabbit's majik, even falters as shockwaves of gravitational force permeate the universe. Watching intently, Poqi adds a forceful blast of dirty-Time into Slothy's majik spell, freezing Gravity's feet for a moment at least—long enough for Feenickz to skedaddle past and escape into a wormhole.

Once Feenickz is gone, Gravity is able to wriggle out of the binding hold of the sloth's spell. He charges out the door. But by then Feenickz and Slothy are long gone. On the wisps of the breeze the wolf can still smell them, though. The scent is faint and hardly a trail, but it's there. He runs after it, ripping up the ground into waves of distorted spacetime.

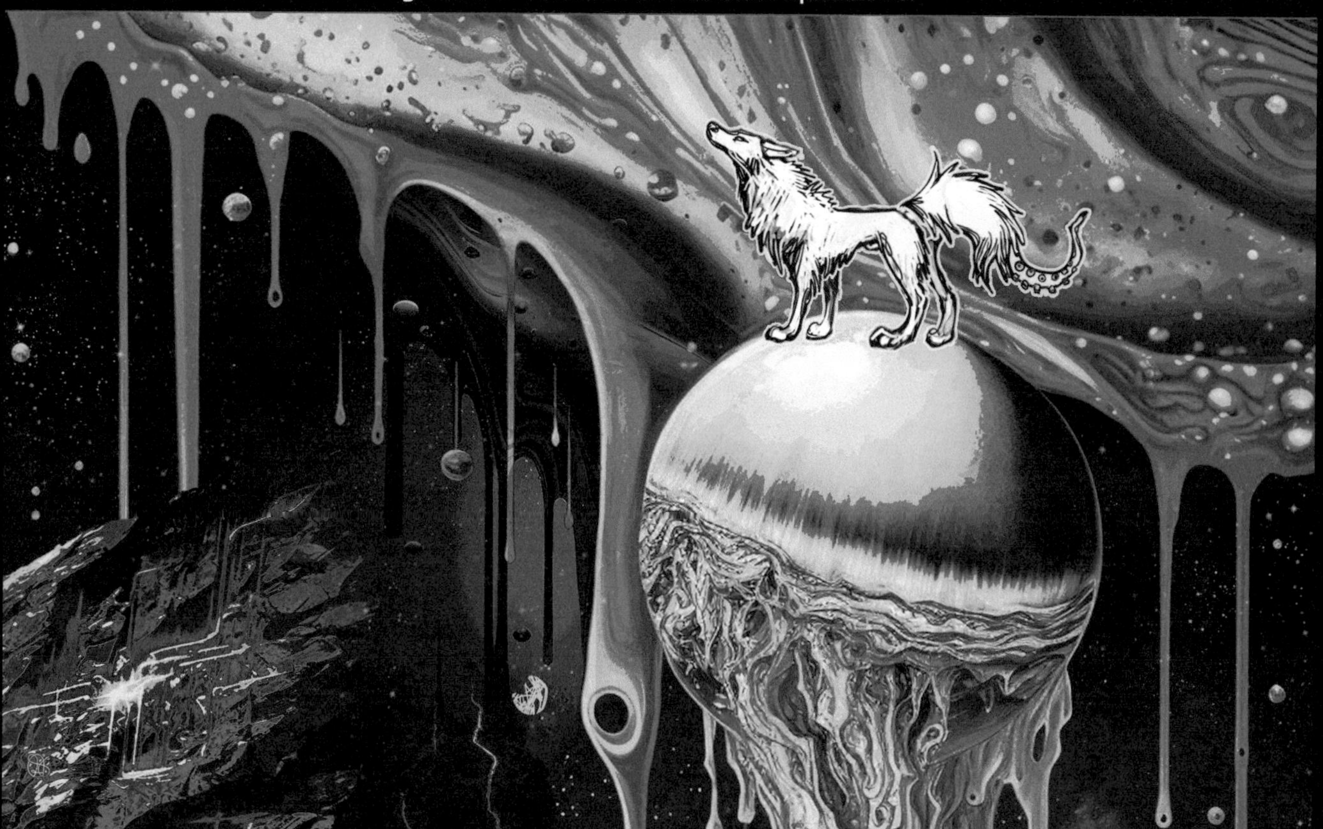

WHAT FUELS FRIVOLITY IS

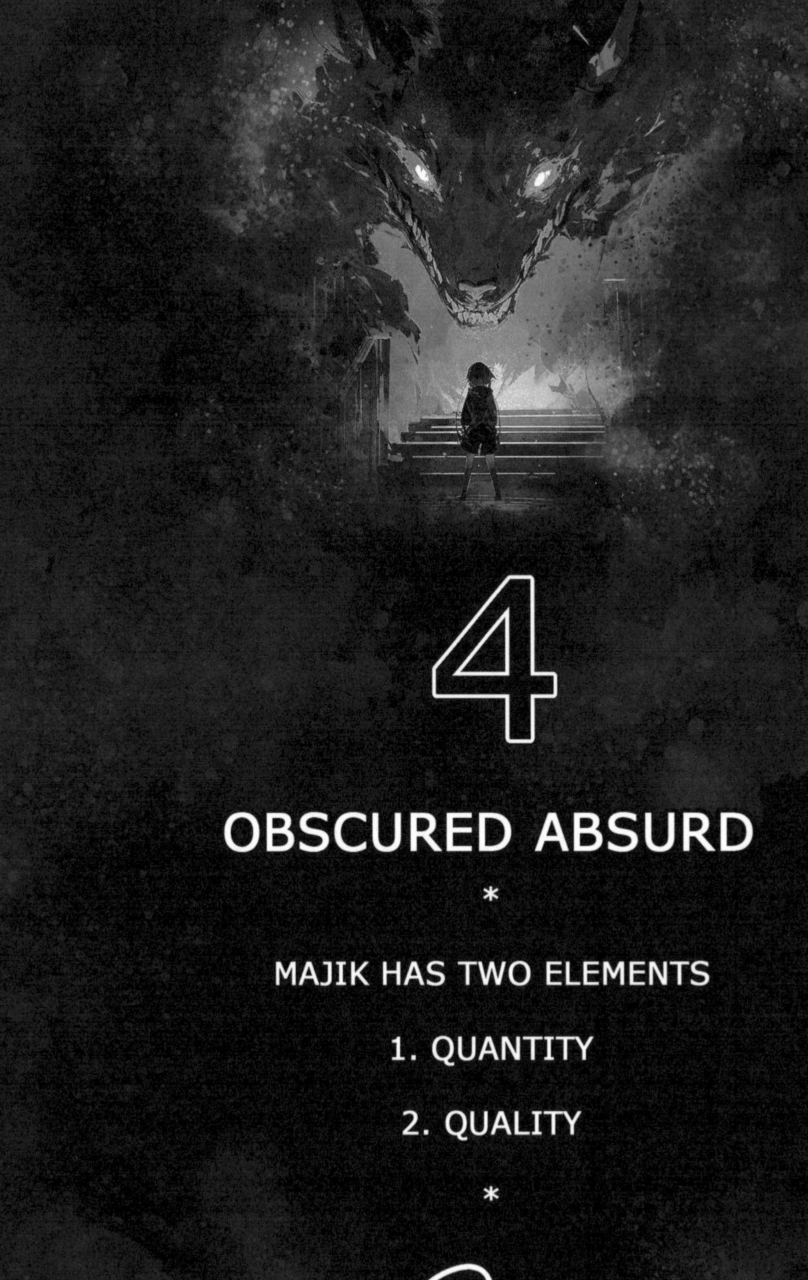

4

OBSCURED ABSURD

*

MAJIK HAS TWO ELEMENTS

1. QUANTITY

2. QUALITY

*

THE DARKNESS IT UNDERMINES

The deeper into the ScarCity you go, the more lavish the buildings become. Along the inner banks of the River of Time are some of the most expensive dwellings in ScarCity, renowned for their spectacular views. But all around the edges of the city, where the river is curbed by the desert, are the poorly kept developments known as the waterfront slums.

In an upscale neighborhood bordering the waterfront resides Bonto, a recently dead pit bull terrier. Though he knew not why—he had always been a good boy—he was disgraced with a negative URO number upon his arrival to the realm of the dead. Those with negative URO numbers have significantly less social power than those with positive ones. Being such, Bonto's options were limited in what he could do from there. He awoke in his new dead state in an animal shelter and was adopted by a somewhat wealthy couple. Yet though his home is decently nice, his people aren't ever there. So Bonto spends his days alone, confined to the fenced yard. He continuously runs stress laps, barking madly at all the gaudy, unused objects.

One day, a horrible scream outside his yard stops him dead in his tracks. The sound incenses him. Bonto repeatedly slams his body against the fence. Though he has never been able to overcome it, still he pushes. Suddenly, a force beneath his paws shimmers like dazzling, soft, elastic lightning—*majik*. It shouldn't have been possible. Since he has a negative URO, he possesses no majik of his own. But there it is. And out he goes.

The sound is coming from Phigher the jackal—her tail had turned completely into fire, burning everything inside her. But Bonto's crashing approach cuts her howl short. The ferocity in his eyes causes Phigher to bolt. As he gives chase, Bonto says nothing except a phrase he snarls inadvertently because his mouth is hung open wide in running stride: "You are myyy-ne."

Bonto chases Phigher through the slums until they are at the river's edge. There is no feasible exit; being that they're in the Afterlife, this chase could be endless. Phigher's tension builds and builds. Suddenly, a whirling warp of dark energy bends the sky high above into a ring. Perhaps this is her calling. Phigher bravely leaps into the air. There, her flaming tail explodes, giving her another jet of propulsion. As the flames are extinguished, what's revealed are the two extra tails it created, giving Phigher the elastic spring to jump higher than she's ever jumped before.

Much to Phigher's chagrin, the other side of her escape ring is not the safe place she was hoping for. The ring portal—a teleportation hole that leads to a random destination—has dumped her right into a wormhole maze. In a confusing matrix of twisting holes such as this, the only way out is through. She picks an especially shiny hole, and falls into the dark void. Little does she know, Bonto has in him a tremendous leap. Fueled by fury, he follows her into the ring portal just before it closes up.